TWELVE TALES FROM

The Repository

of

Lost Souls

JANE ROBERTS-MORPETH

The Repository of Lost Souls

The Repository of Lost Souls

Contents:

The Repository of Lost Souls: Introduction

Welcome to The Repository of Lost Souls. A place for tales – and the people who walk within them – to step inside and rest their weary heads.

Meet the vengeful mermaid, the weary ghost. The sibling vampire and the curious child. Those damaged by war. Join the final journey of the Bone Queen.

'To a rag and a bone and a hank of hair,
(We called her the woman who did not care)'

The Vampire - Rudyard Kipling

Follow the hare. And welcome.

Jane Roberts-Morpeth
Whitley Bay 2019

El Salto del Colacho (The Devil's Jump)

The devil suit is distasteful. Sunflower polyester trimmed with cheap crimson satin that wouldn't look out of place in a brothel.

Rafa pulls it on with distaste and sees the swell of his gut is highlighted by the shoddy cut of the costume. A button succumbs to the bulge and a curl of belly hair emerges.

He struggles to tie the laces on his new white trainers, fearing the rip of the tight yellow fabric across his backside if he bends down too far.

He sucks it all in, marches to the start line at the brow of the hill. An ancient usher hands him a tatty horsewhip and some plastic castanets with a marijuana leaf emblazoned on them.

Rafa has tried to get out of this fiasco. But Yelena stood firm. Wailed about their only child's unprotected soul. Withheld favours until he capitulated. He looks for Rosa, that unblessed soul. His daughter is somewhere in the road below him, on a little blue plastic island waiting for the devil to be discharged.

Rafa is a man of secular beliefs in a town of superstition. He struggles to keep his expression neutral as the red Catholic crows intone and incant. His guts squirm as he waits. He'd thought of feigning bellyache but reasoned that Yelena would see straight through his subterfuge. Now he wonders if he's about to get cosmic payback.

The crimson crows finish their dirge. Mark each runner with holy water. Rafa can't help but notice that Mateo to his right cuts a far finer figure in the polyester monstrosity than he does. And he doesn't seem to have the spreading orange glow about the armpits that Rafa now sports as he waits in the midday sun.

The devil dads are herded forward as the crowd stills. From here Rafa can see the course with its little blue plastic bundles like so many stranded dinghies on the tarmac, each with its own unprotected cargo.

Bile rises in his throat as the church bell begins to clatter. A surge of men moves forward, streaming down towards the village square. The suit chafes Rafa's thighs as he runs and he feels like a fool, but as he begins to gain speed he moves with surprising grace to the head of the field.

The first dinghy comes into view and he sees the balled fists and the angry small face of a child glare at him. Not his Rosa, she must be further down the track. As he comes close, he pushes off the tarmac in his shiny white sneakers and sails over the unfortunate child.

As Rafa lands the world recedes. All there is are the innocent children on their fragile blue boats. Each one aglow, a golden nimbus surrounding their faces.

He feels that light burn his skin. The devil infuses him, makes him nimble as he flies down the road skimming the infants without touching so much as a hair. He is no longer a polyester clown.

He is El Salto, the devil himself, running from the light of these pure souls as the liturgy of the crimson crows floods his ears. He cracks his whip and shakes his castanets to drive the sound of purity away, but it is all consuming, pushing him on, on, on.

Then the road is behind him and Yelena is catching him by the shoulders as she laughs and throws her arms about him. Warm hair pushes into Rafa's nose and makes the world tangible again.

He touches his face, is astonished by the tears he finds there. Retrieves his daughter from her dinghy and wonders how he has never seen the light that flows so strongly through her before.

The Devil is vanquished. The children are pure.

Follow the Hare

Follow the hare! Follow the hare! Twisting, dancing, bucking his dance across the green.

He calls her; teases, beckons her to follow as she watches him with sleepy eyes from the car as it winds up the steep drive to church. Spring blossoms hang across the road, heavy with bright buds that promise pink confetti.

Sunday best, checked dress in the palest of blues. Patent shoes, Mary Jane's toe to toe under the pew as her legs swing above the hassock.

Twitching, impatient to be out. To be running, to follow the hare. The bright day is calling; there are eggs to be found. Sweet nuggets filled with caramel wrapped in precious foil: green, red, silver the colour of Christmas.

She misses the invocation, is late to stand for the prayer. As she does her new blue tights snag the pew and tear. There are parental frowns.

The child is unconcerned. Shiny eggs are in her vision, tucked around the church. Hidden under sunshine yellow toy chicks.

There's a litany; a song of rebirth and redemption, words that twist and dance on the blossom branches that tap the windows, beckoning her *out, out out*. Away on their petals, soft and bruised as they fall.

The words end, the children are released. Most head straight for the indoor fruits, hands eager under the chicks, breaking nests and fake feathers. The girl heads for the door. Out there she gazes clear-eyed across the field, seeking the hare. He's gone now but the blossom is drifting blush snow across the path and she runs, runs for joy down the avenue of trees into the big field where she can see the foil sparkle its primal shades and she can hunt alone for the sweet treasure.

There are pockets in her pretty dress and she crams them with chocolate eggs as her small hands dip into bushes and scrabble behind carved wooden benches. She runs in the meadow, tender green shoots bent beneath the patent shoes as she dances for joy, for spring, for the new life that flows through the earth and the shy flowers that are beginning to emerge in the hedgerow. The girl's hair is full of petals and as she kicks her constraining shoes off into the hedge she feels dew soak into her wool-clad feet.

There are squeals from the church as a crowd of children surge into the meadow. The girl doesn't want to be with them, just wants to dance with the hare. But he's gone and she's at the foot of the old oak tree that spans the centre of the meadow and she's climbing, ripping the cotton tights beyond redemption. Squirrel fingers find tiny knots to cling to as magpies erupt from the crown of the tree in protest.

The dress rips on a fork in the old trunk. The girl perches in her aerie, watching the other children scramble about below. The magpies settle higher up in the tree, watching her pull a silver coated egg from her pocket. Their eyes follow the movement of the foil being peeled back with care, smoothing the wrapper free from crumples.

Raisin eyes watch as she eats the egg, sucking crumbs of chocolate and caramel from fingertips, freckled face sticky with joy. She looks up at them, notices an untidy bundle off twigs and leaves in a cluster of branches to her right.

The girl stands on tiptoes to see eggs in the nest, speckled turquoise brilliant against the brown twigs and moss.

It would be so easy to reach out and touch them. To slip one in her pocket to join the bright chocolates she's harvested from the meadow.

The magpies watch her face. The world slips away below them.

The girl takes the silver foil. It catches the light, and a magpie hops closer, head tilted.

She places it on the branch, moulding it against the bark. Knots and whirls stand out in crisp relief as they catch the light in the dull silver.

The magpie struts a little. Walks closer.

The girl sits back on the fork of the tree. She doesn't smile. She watches the birds.

The magpie reaches the foil. Inspects its own reflection.

Girl and bird; brown eyes and black. They meet once and the girl nods.

Slides down the bark and skins her knees. Let's her mother catch her at the base.

The noise of the world floods back. A child cries, frustrated in their search for the shiny treasure. Behind him the girl sees the bib of a white tail as the hare materialises. Kicks its heels.

Vanishes into the hawthorn.

The girl takes her mother's hand, sinks onto the grass. Squashes an egg as she does so. As laughter bursts about her she looks into the tree where the magpie is strutting towards the nest, silver foil in its beak.

Follow the hare, she thinks, a green foil egg softening in her hand. Follow the hare.

Sister Vampire

Thessaly tells me that she's going to drink my blood.

I ignore her, face wedged against the sticky glass of the café window. The slick glass tastes like salt.

Waves ferment at the edge of the decking below the cafe. Every so often the wind changes direction and sand dances on the decking, pittering against the window. I follow its path whilst my mouth performs the fish dance. Haddock today. I pop my lips.

Thessaly prods my ribs with a sharp pinkie. I focus on her reflection. Her dimples are dollops of ketchup in the glow of the open stove behind us. *Blood, blood, blood*, she's muttering, stamping her little feet in time with her internal rhythm. She's like a blade of grass in her apple green jeans, fists on hips and lips stained with raspberry milkshake.

Behind her our parents read today's newspapers, breakfast plates pushed aside, coated with flakes of brass from cinnamon pastries.

I watch the sea. There's a surfer, tiny in black against a silver avalanche that curls above him as he glides into its fall. His head bobs up seconds later. I wish I could walk on water.

I always knew Thessaly was a vampire. She cultivates scabs. Juicy crusts that form at her knees and elbows. Peeled, devoured and regrown. She works at them patiently, allowing the pink skin underneath to be revealed with exquisite slowness. Then she lays her prize on her tongue, eyes closed in bliss as it dissolves in her saliva.

A gourmet for a ghoul.

She tells me solemnly that she needs it for the metal inside; that it is filled with tiny iron filings that will make her blood better.

Sometimes her wounds don't close as they should. Scarlet outlines the creases on her pale skin.

I tell her to suck on a two pence piece instead. That's iron enough, without all this self-peeling business.

She tells me to go lick more windows.

We're both wearing hats. Mine is knitted in several shades of blue, with a navy pompom perched at a rakish angle on the top of my head. Thessaly's has sideburns and tassels; a riot of purple snakes that curve about her pointy face. You can just about see the snub of her nose from the side.

It's a stupid hat.

The window tastes of the echoes of a thousand fried eggs as I race down it following the path of the surfer. My tongue snags on a lump of grease. I am transfixed as the surfer vanishes for ten heartbeats, before he reappears sleek as a seal at the top of a wave.

I envy him the freedom of the wave and his ability to capture its spirit with his board. He's not being told what to do. He's not been told that he has to miss class tomorrow; miss a trip to an indoor pool where a wave machine throws you at speed round a curving watercourse. Where you can feel what it's like to rush with the water, and ride it.

He isn't going to be tied to a bed with a hook in his leg.

His sister isn't reminding him that your blood belongs to her.

Thessaly yanks at my hat, hot hands covering my ears. I see the ghost of her smile in the glass as she pulls harder.

Monday comes swept clean by yesterday's storms. I don't lick the car windows. My parents spray lemon juice onto them to discourage me. It tastes like the glass in public toilets.

The car keeps pace with a black-headed gull. I'm floating with the bird, rising on the thermals above it all.

Thessaly takes my hand in hers and squeezes it numb. She's staring straight ahead, her face a mask, but I can feel she's scared.

She's a vampire, true, but she is still my little sister.

The nurses coo at me, *brave boy, good lad.* Sweet words don't take away the barb of the needle. They take my blood then leave me lying on a lumpy metal bed.

One wall of the room has floor length windowpanes that are frosted with condensation. I go over to them and track a long strip across the largest pane with my tongue. On the other side there's a ragged garden populated by scarecrow people in rainbow dressing gowns. Lights flare in the drizzle as people smoke, slippers soaking up the damp.

An eyeball meets mine in the glass and I jump as a giantess presses a crusty red cheek to the pane, crushing a cigarette against the glass. It burns like a baleful eye against my pupil. The giant stamps her feet and opens her mouth to wheeze silent laughter. I'm taken with the broken landscape of her teeth.

Just as my tongue extends to poke the window once more, the nurse returns, all brightness and false cheer. She's wheeling Thessaly, a pale doll that resembles those porcelain monstrosities Grandma perches on stands behind untouchable clean glass in her dining room. That glass tastes of time, locked in a prison.

Thessaly isn't porcelain but like some of Grandma's dolls her hair comes away with her hats, leaving dusky cobwebs that drift featherlike around her small skull.

'You're horrible' she says to me. The giantess is capering on the spot behind me, her mouth wide in a tombstone grin.

'I'm not the one drinking other people's blood.'

'Drinking blood?' the nurse echoes. 'There's no drinking of blood here, my loves. We just take a bit in case you need a transfusion, Thessaly. You do have unusual blood.'

Thessaly pulls a face at me. She may look like Grandma's dead dolls, but her eyes are indigo with furious life.

Day zero. Thessaly is stored like a tiny pod child in a gleaming white matchbox of a room. We're gazing through a viewing window watching her doze as she accepts the transfusion. My mouth tastes of dirty glass. I'm mouthing fish faces through her window to try to make her laugh.

There's no response. She floats on a cloud made of cotton, her skin translucent. The blood bag at her side fills the port in her chest her with rusty liquid. *My* liquid. The nurses tell me its full of white cells that will make her well again.

My mother's hands are covered with snot and she won't stop stroking my hair. It's making me cringe but I let her do it because I don't want her to cry again.

I close my eyes and press my face hard against the glass, tongue flattened against it even though it tastes foul.

When I open them again Thessaly is staring at me, indigo eyes massive in her pixie face. She breaks into a weak smile — a sudden starburst of light—, then raises a hand to point at her wicked sharp incisors.

Vampire, she mouths, then points at herself. She raises her other hand and forms a finger heart round the chest port.

My fingers grip the windowsill until they sting. Vampire. Sister vampire.

The very heart of me.

Barflies

There's an adult world they keep from us. Me and my brother, short for our ages, hair cut ragged around old pudding bowls. It tugs us. We smell it through the floorboards — sour and dank and full of promise.

Upstairs our world is woodchip and three-bar electric fires in a vast space that can't be warmed. Afternoon shift done, the landlord sleeps deep in rum.

We venture below; curling toes round the stair spindles as we lower ourselves over the bannister. It brings us up against a thick door. This side there's a Yale lock. My brother is just tall enough to turn it. We hold our breath in case it squeaks.

Pull the door, peep through, then peep behind.

Silence.

He goes first, the eldest. I step behind, toes flexed as my white cotton socks soak up puddles from the lino.

The hall is dim. The window up ahead is paned with glass that is coated tobacco mustard. We take two steps and stop. Two steps and stop. Listen.

Two more steps and we reach a second door chocked back with a wooden wedge. Light spills at the edges, hazy dust spinning crazy stars.

We step through the door onto a riotous carpet – brown, yellow, black squiggles that hurt the eyes if you look too long. Both of my socks are stained and damp now. I peel them off and drop them onto a leather banquette next to the door.

To my left is the piano, lid up, keys beckoning. The strings whisper discord but my brother shakes his head. There's a finger at his lips.

Too much noise, he's saying, as he lifts the hatch to the bar. Rests it against the wall without a sound.

The bar gleams mahogany in the afternoon sun, forming the curving spine of the room. The optics that hang behind it gleam like exposed ribs. I follow my brother, one hand grasping the hem of his school shirt. There's treasure in the ribcage — but danger too.

I check the floor. The cellar hatch is closed. I press my ear to it, hear the buzz of the kegs as they fizz in their dark prison. The cellar scares me and I'm relieved it's padlocked so I don't have to enter the belly of the beast.

When I stand up, I am a head shorter than the bar. I'm level with the sinks, piled high with plastic drip trays on the drainer. There's a rainbow of cordial optics to their side, just below the counter.

My brother has claimed the blackcurrant cordial. This leaves me the lemon, luminous against the counter. I crouch on the floor, mouth open and press my lips to the plastic spout. Push it up and feel the bittersweet tang as liquid fills my mouth. It overspills and spatters my white school shirt.

I point to the mark and my brother shrugs. Sticks his tongue out at me. It's purple. His teeth have become blackened stumps in the dull light.

There are boxes of crisps and nuts behind the counter but they make too much noise to eat. Can't wake Dad. Instead my brother pulls the jar of pickled eggs down from the back counter and we sit cross-kneed on the floor as he screws the top off. Brown vinegar splashes on his fingers. I stick my hand in the jar; grasp an egg through the grubby liquid. It feels squishy as I press it.

'Hurry up!' he hisses, as I sit with my hand in the jar wondering if I really want it. I'll have to eat it all if I do. We can't leave any evidence that we've been here.

I go for it. The egg is rubbery on the tongue and not nice. I can see by his face that my brother thinks the same, his cheeks bulging as he shoves the whole thing in his mouth in one go.

I do the same and choke. He bangs me on the back and I cough the egg into my skirt where it leaves another stain. I wrap the chewed egg in a paper towel and hide it behind the drip trays.

He's bored and heads back into the main bar. I don't like being alone behind here. The beer scented beast threatens to swallow me up and the egg has made me feel sick. I can smell it; on my hands, on my clothes. From the smelly little parcel on the drainer.

Back in the bar we head to the banquettes that line three walls. There are gaps between the base and the back. Drunk people are careless with their cash and money pours behind the seats that only little fingers can reach with ease.

I'm the smallest. So, in I go, the tunnel sour with spilled beer. Peanuts crunch under my bare knees. My feet are filthy as I swarm along on my belly harvesting notes and coins. I push them out to my brother as I worm my way around the wall.

He gathers the money and counts it out into equal piles. At least I think it's even. He counts better than me, but today I think he has more paper notes than I do. He counters this by pushing silver coins at me. It's best not to argue. He's bigger than me and could take it all if he wanted.

Still, I did all the work finding it. And he's clean, when I'm dirty from head to toes, and in big trouble when Mam gets back from the shops

I shove the cash in my skirt pocket.

Sun streams in through the plate glass windows that curve round the front of the room. We sit on the floor watching shadows pass. My stomach squeaks. I want peanuts but they are high on the wall, higher than even my brother can reach.

The windows are framed with thick velvet curtains, a rich red full of dust that makes me sneeze when I shake them. The window ledge is wide and holds games: dominos, playing cards, a scrabble board, lidless pens. I point to the dominos but he shakes his head.

'Too noisy' he mouths. Instead he takes a beer mat, strips the back off it to give him a clear square and begins to draw in blue biro.

I sit beside him and shake my head when he offers me a beer mat. He's engrossed as he draws a tank with stick figure soldiers carrying out a bloody battle. He doesn't notice when I twist and reach up to the sill to get a pack of cards.

I catch a wooden box of dominos with a careless thumb. The crash of them falling echoes around the bar and we freeze, two small figures huddled against a tatty banquette.

I see the fear in my brother's eyes and I know it's reflected in mine. At first there is silence. Just as it stretches into the point of safety, a noise reaches us.

A creak overhead. The crash of a door.

My brother grabs my hand, pulls me up. Holds a curtain and motions for me to stand behind it, visible from the street but hidden in the bar. He takes the opposite curtain, twitches it into place around his feet. Feet that are slightly longer than the window is wide.

Just in time. We hear the bull roar, the heavy step. Anger surges into the air before the man comes through the door.

We stand still as statues, twin sentries at their post.

Silence. Our father blunders about and curses our names but he hasn't spotted us. Not sure if we were even here or if he's been woken by a rum cursed dream.

I hear him turn to leave the bar. Relief brings a grin at my brother who is staring ahead, his lips pressed together and his hair square about his face.

I look at my feet and wonder why they are bare.

Hear my father stop at the banquette by the door. Pick something up.

Our world falls.

Blood Poppies
(Twinned with The Memory Tin)

I broke the bread bowl. I tried to hold it in childish arms that had little strength, thinking only to help my mother. But the great pottery dish slipped and fell onto the flagstones. It exploded into a haze of flour and clay chips, my guilt dressing me pallid for all to see. Ma cried out at the crash, eyes sharp with shock as the flour fanned evidence of my folly to dust her heels.

Neither of us moved as we heard the slow hitch of steps on the wooden boards of the hall; step, thud, step, thud.

The secret snake in my stomach danced and hissed as Da materialised in the doorway. I couldn't raise my eyes, couldn't look away from the mess I'd created even as he spoke my name.

'Anne.'

He rolled my name like a disappointment. Ma shuffled back against the kitchen units.

'Oh Anne, what have you done?'

The harsh sorrow in his voice undid me. Tears fell. I risked a glance at him, bottom up from the thick-soled shoes and third leg. I gazed past britches that hung in folds from his wasted body as he balanced on the curved head of his stick. The tang of bitter rum was strong even at a distance, the spirit sweated into the pits of his shirt.

I grabbed my pinny with anxious fists, fingers curled into the rough cotton.

There was a murmur from the counter, Ma's rasp of a voice. 'She's just a child, Lewis.'

'She's ten. Old enough to have some care.'

Inside I felt all needles. He called to me again, and I forced a tentative step forward, arching my bare foot over the debris to a clear patch of floor.

'Walk in a straight line, Anne.' His voice was mild, but as I raised my chin to gaze at him, I saw his face set in unforgiving lines.

The path before me was smothered with shards of clay. *Feet of clay, fingers of mud,* my mind whispering, as I looked to my Ma. No help there, she was crouching behind the kitchen table, clutching her own mixing bowl tight to her skinny chest.

There was a light in my Da's eyes, bright like the flare of the guns that took his health and shot his reason. There was no mercy. Just the flame of fury.

I stepped onto the chaos of the broken bowl.

Pain twisted my bare foot; bubbles in my mouth, a sick tang. My chin drooped, a coil of saliva spiraled towards my chest. Not looking up, only tiny steps from tile to tile as the blood from my feet created a crimson ballet of dancing footprints curly toed in the flour.

It helped to concentrate on the movement. Of placing one foot before the other until I stood before Da.

He loved me once, I know. From the tatters of the letters of war that remain, filled with *my darling* this and *don't forget me, my beautiful girls*. Somewhere out there he lost us.

He was clutching a tin. Battered brass. His Mary tin he called it. A gift full of cigarettes from a grateful princess, given to soldiers as a thank you. Now filled with the sweet morphia that coated his tongue and his judgement, washed down with cheap gin and bitter memories.

His thumb caressed Princess Mary's head, Brimful of sweet Morpheus, he would say. He carried it in his shirt pocket. Held over his heart.

Sweet Morpheus had swung towards my face, Da driving the metal edge of the tin into the meat of my chin. A hiss of a scream from Ma from the back of the kitchen. A repeat of the blow.

My feet were numb. I managed a clumsy shove to Da's stick. He crumpled to the floor, dropping his tin. Mary burst open, her brass corner folding as she scattered her nectar on the floorboards. My father squealed, part rage, part wounded child.

My bare toes dug into the tiles and I began to run. To run and not look back, only down as blood from my chin spattered irregular drops onto my skirt.

Blood poppies blossomed on cream *broderie anglaise.* Later they would fade to pale yellow, much as the scar on my chin faded to silver.

A permanent echo to fear.

The Memory Tin

My knotty hands fasten of their own volition onto the box. I call the blue twists River Danube. It amuses my grandchildren, but I can't bear them, these tunnels that expose my secret insides. Their fragility scares me.

There's a butterfly trapped in the corner of the kitchen window. Caught in the net, it beats a frantic tempo with wings of scarlet and tiger's eye. I watch it struggle; listen to the echo of its wings reverberating across the vaults of my memory.

I follow the wing beats through these grey rooms, expanses of emptiness that grow ever wider, pockmarked with ghosts. I have no instructions, no guide to these paths of the past; the blue print is too faded.

I hold the tin. Its solidity reassures; whispers of a history illustrated on my skin. There was a man who took the perfection of my face in his rage. As my thumbs caress the edge, the right one snags on the dent in the outer casing and draws blood.

There's a sudden *slam* and the present catches me unawares.

'Mum? Are you home?' Esther strides into my kitchen and hugs me, the warm sphere of her body drawing me back to the now. I'm still by the window, the tin dropped in the sink as the tap flows. Crimson outlines the Princess's face.

'Mum? You ok?' There's concern in the girl's voice. I pin on my reassuring smile as I turn to meet her.

'Just cut myself on this old tin.' I hold my thumb out for inspection; really the cut is of no account, a shallow graze in the groove of a joint.

The butterfly has stilled behind the net. Esther makes me a cup of tea, the sweetness of honey added to combat the shock that she insists I must be feeling. She fusses too much but it's nice to be cared for.

'I don't know why you keep this tin. You can't keep anything in it' she says. She takes it from the sink and places it on the drainer.

She doesn't know it gave me the pink ridge on my chin. Or that it is the space in which I lay the memories of a man who couldn't run from his own. I prefer it that way. Her grandfather died long before her birth, lost to a war he was called to fight in, but could never win. Better she thinks of him as a hero painted in sepia, a jaunty army cap tilted to the camera as he smiles my own lopsided smile.

The sun sparkles into the kitchen and catches the brass tin. It illuminates the dead princess's smile. Mary, I think. Her name was Mary.

Above the sink the butterfly resumes its panic.

Esther takes a glass and floats the blowsy wings inside, careful not to damage them. The butterfly shivers, eyes perpetual motion as she opens the window and shakes it free. She holds the net back, smiling at me.

'See? He's found your buddleia. And his friends.'

It's true. There is a cluster of brilliance flitting amongst the purple cones, a kaleidoscope of amber wings. We sit together at the old kitchen table and watch the summer. The tin is forgotten.

For now, there is only the summer and it dances in my daughter's eyes.

Longshanks and Lavender

Scott watches the pet cemetery. Imagines the occupants staring back with bright eyes from hollow skulls. Sketches a zombie-Bambi onto his revision notes.

He sits in the box room breeze, at a right angle to his desk, feet on the sill of the sash window. He likes this view across Northumberland Park. Likes the quiet dead. It's the living he has trouble with.

Exams hang over his desk as Scott watches spring unfurl from his window. Blossom falls, pink, cream, lavender confetti that dances over the small graves and drifts in his window. It reminds him of Lila's hair and the bright colours that spin into frothy tails as she walks.

There's an old man sleeping against the park's boundary wall in the shade of the copper beech hedge, hat tipped over his face. Scott can hear children playing laughing, screaming.

He's thinking about Lila again. The dimple in her right cheek. Amber eyes, dark lashes. How her hair glows against her black jacket and the perfect curve of her body.

Behind him the breeze gets mischievous and scatters his history notes, forcing him to catch them as they fly for the open window. Point taken universe, he thinks. Turns. Settles back to Corn Laws and Potato Famines.

Later the sun flows across Scott's desk, framing his bony shoulders in golden streamers. His hair falls in a curtain of caramel curls that shield his eyes from the glare.

He reads his textbooks, types notes, works through example questions. Ignores sudden shouts from beneath his window. The same tired insults, unimaginative abuse. Words like *beanpole* bounce off him with indifference. He likes being tall.

The idiots are persistent and a quick glance at their bovine faces tells him they've settled into the cemetery with several large green bottles of oblivion. Tomorrow morning the empties will be scattered on the grass like deflated skittles and Scott will put them in the bin before walking to school.

He clicks a playlist at random, puts on his headphones and screens out the world with guitar noise. Studies until his mother calls him down for tea.

As he shuts his window, he notices the old man has gone from the hedge. The idiots are still there, sitting on Bambi's grave.

At ten past eight Lila walks down Park Avenue. Scott catches a flash of candy-floss hair and turns from his notes to watch her. He wills her to look up, to see him.

She doesn't look up. She never does. For a year she's lived twelve doors down from him. Passed by his house, his window. Lila never looks up. Never waves. Never smiles. Just floats on past with her big purple headphones in place.

Rumour tails Lila. About family disgrace, her father in prison and the family moving north to get away from scandal. Scott sees none of this. He just sees the pale cheeks and the dimples. Admires her self-possession.

At school she drifts on the edges of cliques disinterested in sixth form politics. She reads books while eating apples. Like Scott she moves in a headphone-induced cloud of music between lessons. He'd think her a blank page if he hadn't seen her in the creative writing class they take together on a Monday lunchtime.

He thinks that's where he fell in love with her, that first session when she pulled an old notebook from her backpack. Read lines of poetry that she punctuated with her glitter nails, mascaraed lashes falling over her own words. Where she'd brought Scott to the verge of tears so often that he would lose his nerve when his turn to read came around.

Scott writes appalling sonnets addressed to a purple -haired maiden. Her indifference only appears to grow.

Scott is watching Lila that night as she walks by the park. Sees her interest caught, her headphones removed. As he follows her line of sight, he hears the shouting, the pleading sobs of a victim. His stomach twists inside.

He wills Lila to keep walking away from trouble. Instead she hops over the beech hedge, stashes her backpack behind a bush then marches towards the pet cemetery. Her canvas shoes flash white at her heels. Scott can see the same mob that had been beneath his window earlier crowding round a curled figure on the grass. He hopes someone else sees the trouble from the street. Calls the police, goes to help her. He doesn't want to be brave.

The figure tries to pull itself upright as the group surrounds it. Scott sees it is the old man he saw asleep earlier. He's wearing a bright coat that seems to move as he jerks himself upright.

Lila must have shouted because the mob turns in her direction. Everyone is still for a moment. Then they circle her. Scott runs through his house and out of the front door that he leaves wide open behind him.

Scott doesn't want to be a hero. But he can't leave Lila on her own, one small soul against three. So he doesn't think about his bare feet as he jumps the wall and sprints across the cool grass. He doesn't have a plan. He just runs into trouble with his skinny fists balled.

Scott runs to save the girl.

The girl is quite capable of saving herself.

Scott finds Lila unleashing scorn on the would-be attackers. As he draws level, he sees she has a coffee cup in her hand. The ringleader moves to attack. Receives a face full of latte. He stumbles over a tiny grave hidden in the long grass, falls onto his face.

Behind him Scott hears the old man wheeze a laugh, his coat tinkling with the movement. As Scott comes closer, he sees that the old man's coat is covered in hundreds of tiny shells.

Lila is a pale warrior with a lavender halo. She unclips the chain that she is wearing through the belt loops of her jeans and swings it with intent, fully focused on the old man's attackers.

Scott hears sirens wail and his relief is immense. He doesn't have to be a hero. It is enough to stand beside Lila. As the sirens get louder, the old man claps his hands over his ears and begins muttering to himself. The music from his shells becomes discordant.

A tall stocky girl with a lip ring yanks Ringleader to his feet and drags him across the cemetery where she shoves him over the wall. A short boy in a grey tracksuit fumbles along behind.

Lila never drops her predatory gaze as they run. As Scott wonders where she learned to be so fierce, two policemen lumber over the beech hedge towards them — the lavender haired warrior, the barefoot boy and the shell-coated oldie.

The attackers crash towards the park's pond. Lila slides her chain into her jacket pocket, turns to smile at the policemen. She is charm personified as she gestures to the old man in his coat of many shells. He smiles at her with delight. 'Longshanks and lavender!' he laughs.

'Officers. I'm so glad you're here. This gentleman was being attacked. They ran towards the pond.'

The police are portly and don't seem keen on chasing thugs. They do seem keen to talk to Lila. She speaks rapidly, telling them what happened.

The shorter policeman notices Scott's bare feet, points at them. 'What happened there?'

Scott points at his house where his mother is standing anxiously on the doorstep. 'I live there, ran over. Didn't have time for shoes. There's my mum.'

'You won't mind if we go to your mum's house and take some details?'

'You're not going to chase them?' Lila sounds ferocious.

'Long gone. But we'll take a note and you call us if they come back.'

The taller policeman looks around. 'Where's the old fella gone?'

The shell-coated man has vanished. The police shrug, shoo Lila and Scott towards his mother. As Scott steps over the hedge, he looks round at the cemetery. Under a horse chestnut tree he sees a large rock covered in what looks like limpet shells. He's never noticed it before. His mother is shepherding everyone into the house. Lila looks at Scott, her lips quirking upwards.

Scott forgets the old man. Follows Lila into his house.

Later Lila refuses Scott's offer to walk her home. Instead she gives him her mobile number; takes his in return. He gives her a special ring tone.

Hours later that ringtone blasts him from sleep. A text, in capitals:

'LOOK OUT THE WINDOW!! NOW!!!'

He stumbles out of bed, fights with his curtains and manages to open the sash. Lila is below next to the front wall. Grinning.

It takes a moment to focus on the small front garden. Then he has to check he is actually awake. There are shells everywhere, pearly whelk shells, craggy limpets and pristine white scallops. Words have been picked out on the white paving stones with the sharp black of razor clams.

'Thank you! Shellycoat'

Lila is laughing, hair floating pink in the dawn light. Scott smiles.

'How beautiful you are' he murmurs.

Nymphae and Neridae

Neridae heard soft melody drift through the trees. Choral voices, multifold and soaring, a haunting melody that pulled her from our pool. Turned her face from our waterfall towards humanity. Pulled her tail into limbs.

I heard only discord.

I followed her as she sought the voices, naked through the wood. As we came to its end, she draped herself in a cloak of ivy and followed the path to the village. I followed, fear making my unfamiliar limbs twist and stumble. Heard the sound of our pool fading behind us.

We were untethered. Neridae was seeking new mooring.

We were twins, she and I. Pale flesh made mirror, her eyes moss bright, a shade lighter than mine. The barest distinction, she was my reflection and I hers. She made my contentment.

Reflection can be misleading. Her thoughts did not echo mine. She did not care to share her dreams, her desires with me. I never thought to ask if her dreams differed.

Neridae betrayed me.

For *him*.

We are immortal born. But it comes at a cost. I guard my heart well. No love will pierce my scales. No flesh will touch these lips. My diadem of eels warns the unwary and the bold alike to hold their kisses, their pathetic embraces.

My sister followed that sound. They call us sirens when we sing but the truth is that music holds more sway over our kind than that of humans. She followed it to a wooden building with tall windows and a white spire. It reeked of man.

No water here, no pools to charm. No fish to tickle, no place to drown the unwary. My Neridae was drowning in air.

I watched her float through great arched doors. My beautiful sister, her hair an emerald waterfall, tangled on her cloak of ivy.

I crept behind her, hid in shadow as she stood behind the congregation in a shaft of ruby light. In these man made walls she was beauty made flesh, ethereal and eternal.

As she raised her voice to join the ghastly choir, the humans turned. Fell silent. The men in rapture; women in fear.

Then one stepped forward who I will not name for his name is a curse and should not be spoken alongside my sweet sister's. Tall he was, as fair of face as a human can be. And my sister was lit in rapture as he lifted his voice in song with hers. Enticed her into his arms with harmonies that only they could hear.

With a song my sister was lost to me.

I am solitary now, my pool quiet without her voice to blend with mine. I use my days to entice the pink creatures into my waters. They try to catch me, these sons of Adam with cold grasping hands and hard faces, and I play the coquette to their entitlement.

And I lure them in for that elusive kiss. They see my eels too late, feel them tightening on their fragile spines as I draw them beneath the surface. Hear them gasp as they try to pull away from my embrace.

Snared by desire and a fair face.

As their breath fades and they reach a zenith of despair, my eels tighten to give mercy. I show them their fragile mortality — their gift to my sister. For if her human is unfaithful to her, she will perish — perish like the fools who litter my pool with their cold flesh and blank eyes.

Yet still the men come.

I sing.

Of the sisters Nymphae and Neridae.

Private 48169

The end began with a feather. A perfect downy dove's caress, a creamy oval that the girl gave you at church. You recall the weather; a day of sullen sunshine tempered by gentle winds that transformed the girl's hair into a blond halo as she approached you like an angel. Bearing an angel's wing.

You struggle to remember her name, down here in the mud. One of the Strathmore sisters, Hettie. The name slips away as you open your eyes to the sky, the rain pattering gently down your cheek.

Featherlike.

Private 48169, that's your designation. Here you are indistinguishable from the thousands of others, a dun speck against a blasted landscape that cradles you as you fight the urge to drift. Hettie had green eyes, tilted to the skies and a dimple that creased her mouth as she frowned. Despite her solemnity, you could see the beauty of the woman to come, and you'd watched her with reverence every Sunday from the back pew of the church for many months.

It stung, her insinuation of cowardice. Born late 1900, you were a slight youth, already a veteran miner of two years, following generations of your family before you. As Hettie pressed the feather into your unresisting palm, you couldn't find the voice to tell her that you were only sixteen, too young, too small to pass of age.

Early one Saturday morning, you'd borrowed your Dad's flat cap and laced your mining boots tight. Scrubbed the coal dust from your coarse hands and thick hair and shook the creases from your overcoat. Recruitment was taking place four miles way, so you hitched a lift on the milk cart where the taciturn driver gave you free milk and an apple when he heard your purpose.

'England needs lads like you,' he'd grunted.

And pride at his words had lifted your shoulders, gave you the swagger you needed to convince the recruiting sergeant you were truly eighteen. Truth is, he barely glanced at you. The supply pool of fresh soldiers for war had dwindled considerably by 1917, and there was no hesitation as he scribbled your recruitment papers assigning you both rank and number. A nominal home with the 12th Battalion Yorkshire Regiment.

You've been drifting, here in the mire, wondering why the world has become strangely muted. Travelling home from recruitment clutching your papers you'd been fizzy with excitement. There's a similar sensation in your head right now, but it's not pleasant anticipation. More a sense of wonder, a detachment from your own body which no longer obeys your commands as you watch the bright flares of war dancing across the star-peppered microcosm of a Belgian spring sky.

The memories are becoming hazy. Images rush through your mind as you smile at the stars, the reek of the septic ground beneath your body fading as you dance on that distant pinprick of light. The parade ground at Catterick, with the tight faces of the men who'd returned with Blighty wounds, left to teach you the ropes as you flung yourself into your new life with enthusiasm. Their silence when pressed by young men eager to find glory on the battlefield; reluctant to feed your patriotic zeal.

They'd told you there were rats big as cats, idle chatter as you'd worked hard to master the knack of assembling a Lewis gun faster than any of the lads who cheerfully rubbed shoulders with you. Working in the pit you were accustomed to rodents, not a problem. They hadn't told you the rest. That the rats were nurtured on the rotting carcasses of warhorses, piled high at the side of the trenches. That the sandbags topping the trenches would act as pavements for them to navigate, foraying into the precious tiny space of your bunkroom, gleefully destroying the chocolate sent by your mother that Christmas.

Your mother. Briefly there is respite from your bodily hurts. Her tense face, chin lifted bravely as she waved you goodbye at the station, clutching your regulation uniformed photograph in her white gloves. No sign of Hettie; just a stream of prematurely grieving mothers and wives, the muted sobs of children. Your mother stands before you then, and as you gaze at the sky you mimic the wink you gave her, that jaunty smile for your own comfort as you think of her work-roughened hands and the whip-sharp tongue that hides a gentle nature. For a moment, as you lie in the filth of war, you feel terribly young again, the sharp tang of fear coating your teeth and swarming needles into your stomach.

The names of those you have loved has gone, receded with the night sky as the clouds clear and leave a universe of lights to play on your face as your breath becomes shallower. There's mud in your mouth, on your face, in what remains of your clothing. There is no rescue. The white knights are all dead or diseased and their noble steeds are frozen in mortis all around you. The artillery is getting closer; the battlefield has no name for you. Ypres, Somme, Maretz, Ploegsteert. They've all been fought; all have their unknown soldier whose physical remains have simply been absorbed by the land they fought for. A thousand, tens of thousands of young souls forever lost to their grieving families.

As the shells come closer, you can see the gunpowder flares melding with the stars, creating comets of astounding beauty that you can almost touch, they are so close. Until one surrounds you completely in its purifying whiteness and like the feather gifted to you from gentle hands with determined intent, you float gently skywards, ash and bone on the wind.

Written in memory of my Great Uncle Michael Maughan Renwick, died 11th April, 1918 at Ploegsteert, Belgium, aged 17.

The Carousel Queen

We stood in the shadow of the Dome, my face flushed and my eyes red with tears as you patted my shoulder.

I had tried to be discreet. Tried not to let you see the awful after-effects of strawberry milkshake with a lemonade fizz combined with an aggressive waltzer attendant who had insisted on spin after spin after spin until my stomach had ricocheted into action.

Now there was vomit on my white pants. A patina of pink on your pristine black brogues.

I'd tried to push you away from me as I ran down the stairs, almost tripping until I stood before the Dome while her dancing ladies laughed at me from their frozen pirouettes.

Behind me, the Spanish City trilled and wheezed, a cacophony of music and engine noise. Hawkers paraded along the seafront with trays full of sticky lollipops, bags of cotton candy and paper bags of winkles to be eaten with a sprinkle of salt and a pin.

'Buy a bag for your girl!' one bright spark cried, stepping in front of me and waving an odious bag at you. You declined with decorum as I reeled back, assaulted by the scent.

I sank onto a bench that faced out to sea. You sat beside me and I could see you fighting a smile. You looked so handsome, in your white open neck shirt, hair brushed back from your temples where one unruly curl had fought free to hang over your indigo eyes.

An older lady sat at my other side, squeezing me up uncomfortably against you. She saw my red eyes and messy legs and fished in her handbag to give me a tissue.

'Cheer up, duck. It'll wash out.'

I thanked her but I was thinking that the memory wasn't quite so easy to scrub from the mind. Our first date, punctuated with pink vomit.

You offered to get me a glass of water from the café in the corner of the Dome. I shuffled along the bench, stretched my spine and gazed over the sugar-capped waves to the horizon, the breeze lifting my spirits a little.

'Tuppence they charged me!' You were furious as you handed me a chipped blue mug with the ghosts of a thousand tea leaves littering its inner walls. I gulped it down anyway, thankful it was cool.

You sat beside me again. 'Nice view, Sylvia.'

It was. I sat the blue mug between us. 'It is. I'm sorry, Matty. I shouldn't have had so much pop.'

You smiled a little, turned those indigo eyes to me. 'You did tell me you didn't like the waltzer. And you wanted to go on the carousel.'

'But the queue was too long.'

'Next time, I'll listen to you.'

'Next time?' There was a little glow in my stomach that had nothing to do with any lingering sickness.

'If you promise not to drink milkshake before the rides.' Your smile was broader now, and I noticed the smattering of freckles across your nose crinkle.

'I like Babycham.'

You gave that great belly laugh of yours. Just then it was new and it made me tingle to the tips of my ponytail.

'Babycham it is' you promised. 'But only if you give me that yellow ribbon from your hair.'

I reached round and pulled it free, a pretty length of sunshine that I placed on your upturned palms.

I remembered that ribbon the day you did buy me Babycham in the champagne bar. Up high in the Dome, sheltering from a day of storm and thunder, you handed me the dished glass with the tiny leaping-deer motif.

The Babycham sparkled in the glass and I sipped it, noting how the deer smiled at me with delight as I spun on my tall stool in a pretty polka dot dress.

I was watching the lightning play about St Mary's Lighthouse as you fumbled in your pocket.

'Sylvia?'

'Huh?' I turned my stool to face you, feeling cute as a button in my patent leather Mary Jane shoes fastened with red ribbons to match the one in my hair.

You shocked me by getting on one knee, a little box tied with a yellow ribbon clutched in your left hand. I squealed, causing everyone to look round and a collective *aah* to echo about the room.

You couldn't find the words but you popped the box open to show me the sparkling solitaire sat on dark green velvet. Thrust it towards me.

'Yes, Yes, Yes!'

I confess, I sounded a little smug as you slipped it onto my engagement finger.

People began to clap and a waiter sent over two more glasses of Babycham on the house to toast our engagement with. You hate Babycham but gritted your teeth and smiled through the taste. I was becoming quite giddy.

When you regained your voice, you whispered in my ear. 'I still owe you a ride on the carousel.'

The weather was awful now, rain coming down in fat pennies against the windows, lightening riding in on thunderhead clouds. I didn't care as you took my hand to run down the steps to the Spanish City.

The carousel was at a standstill, as empty as the fair around us in the pelting rain. The operator was supping from a hip flask as we knocked on the door to the control booth. He looked unimpressed to see us laughing in the rain, begging him for a turn in the gloom.

You handed him several notes and he became less grumpy, cranking up the engine. Lights flickered like rainbows as we choose our horses, mine cream with a gold mane. Her name was painted on the proud bow of her neck.

Louisa. So pretty. I ran my fingers across the letters as the carnival music began and we were spun into a wonderland of light and shade as the storm broke above us and we held hands across the space between our horses.

You called to me and your face was brilliant, halo'd under a bright pink bulb.

We named her Louisa, our firstborn. For her golden hair and creamy skin like that of my carousel horse. Every time we say our daughter's name, I think of that ride, and of thunderclouds illuminated by a rainbow of lights, and the joy that filled our hearts as our life together began.

And the Carousel Queen rides again.

The Consequential Hand

Carrie is wired as she steps into the church hall. Her skin buzzes and sweat breaks out on her top lip. She's reluctant to be here, knows that she has to be and yet she can't help but resent the need.

She's deliberately early. She has no idea what to expect or who she is going to be forced to spend the next ninety minutes or so with. Being first will allow her to pick the most unobtrusive seat and recede into the background of this nightmare she finds herself in. As she scans the room, Carrie realises that the dozen or so chairs for the meeting are set in a perfect circle in the centre of the room under bright fluorescent strip lights that leave no shadows.

Panic swells her throat and she steps to the side of the hall to rest her face against the dirty cold pane of glass stretching from shoulder height up into the vaulted ceiling. She breathes deeply, watching her breath mist the glass. It's cold in the hall and there is a metallic tang to the air, scented with the trapped echoes of previous visitors: the taint of the AA meeting, the heat of the Tumble Tots group.

She almost wishes she were here for an AA meeting; it would be so much simpler an addiction to explain. She drops her eyes to her hands impeccable in cream leather gloves that grasp the windowsill. On one hand, the fingers grip a little less tenuously than the other and she raises them both before her face in their suede cladding, gazing at them with a wondering despair.

The gloves themselves illustrate a point. Italian leather, butter soft and creamy. Exquisite mother-of-pearl detailing at the cuffs. The price of a month's heating bills.

She has to do that now. Mentally evaluate the worth of the goods she sees as actual expenditure. To make it finite, absorb the reality of what it is she is taking. She finds that when it comes to gloves her restraint is limited as she seeks to shield her guilty hands from curious eyes.

If she tells herself the truth — and she does on occasion — she hides her hands because gazing at them causes pain inside so great that she feels she may fall into its void.

There's a clattering behind her and Carrie turns to see a tall woman bearing down on her. The other woman is smiling, a little dishevelled, hair sprung and rumpled but there's a kindness in her face that helps Carrie unbend a little.

'Here for the session, love? '

Carrie nods, her tongue snake twisting as she tries to speak. Fails.

The woman pats her arm briskly. 'I'm Eileen, the coordinator. Get yourself a cup of tea from the kitchen. There's biscuits, too. Custard creams do wonders for the nerves.'

Carrie falls obediently into step behind Eileen. Takes a paper cup, fills it with bitter black coffee from a tall flask and liberally adds sugar. Picks up an obligatory custard cream and then looks at both items clutched in two identically gloved hands with consternation. Her right hand is cramping again. She places the biscuit on the edge of the kitchen counter and flexes her fingers within their soft gloved skin. Feels a little better.

More people are entering the hall. Eileen goes to greet them and Carrie follows, taking a seat as close to the window as she can find. There's noise, nervous laughter. A stamping of feet and shaking of coats: apparently, it's raining outside and people have been caught in the downpour. Carrie looks down at her own immaculate cream mac. Matches the gloves. The thought causes her mouth to twist sourly. She sits rigid: custard cream in her right hand, coffee in her left. A little paper doll, like the magazine cut-outs that she used to dress as a child. Dolls with little folds of paper to hold the clothes in place. There was no substance behind the clothes and she knows how easily torn the fabric of paper dolls can be.

The people coming into the hall are all shapes and ages but there's an informal uniform of sorts: jeans and t-shirts for the men, leggings for the women. All cast quick looks at the young woman in her cream coat and matching gloves with the paper-doll smile pinned tight to her face.

Eileen takes charge, brings the circle to order with a clattering of her chair. People are still watching Carrie who is now sick of holding the cup and biscuit. She tries to take a bite of the biscuit and chokes on the dry crumb. Her right hand goes into spasm again and as she clutches at her wrist with the left, her coffee spills across her mac. It soaks into the pristine gloves.

Everyone's noticed her now. There is nowhere to hide. Carrie peels off the left glove, goes to unfasten her coat. Fumbles with the buttons and admits to herself that the right glove also has to come off.

The treacherous right hand flexes again, beyond her mastery. Hers for so short a time. The misery it has caused seems timeless.

Carrie loosens the pearl button, flips the cuff inside out. The gloves are ruined. She's zoning out the faces around her, concentrating on pulling each finger gently as she shakes the glove a little slacker. Carrie removes the glove and places both hands on their corresponding knee.

Both have beautifully painted nails in rich magenta. Squared off with blunt white tips. She paints them to practice her right-handed coordination. To make the hand feel and react as if she were born with it.

There the similarities end. Carrie's own skin is pale, speckled lightly with freckles. Her left hand blends with her skin.

The right does not. The skin is sun kissed olive, the fingers longer and more elegant than those of the left. Carrie wears no jewellery on this hand; she can't bear it. She can barely bring herself to paint her nails.

They told her she'd accept it. Come to see it as part of her. Yet the hand remains estranged from the rest of her body; an alien preserved by a cocktail of drugs well beyond its predetermined natural life.

They told her she was lucky to find such a closely matched donor. A new hand, a new wrist. A complex network of blood vessels and capillaries tied together by a surgeon in unnatural alchemy.

No history. She has asked. Initially for curiosity and then in desperation. She knows where her original — unremarkable — right hand went. Crushed beneath the wheels of the bin lorry her bike had skidded into the path of. Really, she'd taken that corner too fast trying to outrun it, filled with righteous road anger at being cut up.

Big mistake.

So when they'd offered her a replacement option, it seemed heaven sent. The perfect panacea. She'd seen folks wheeled out on the media with much more complex operations, greater transplants than hers. A hand was minor in comparison.

She'd be able to get back on her bike after the operation.

The hand had other ideas.

It was subtle at first. She'd get home and find small items in her pockets. Scarlet nail polish, a chocolate bar. She'd be puzzled about the provenance but then dismissed it. Must have picked them up at work or on her lunch.

The items grew. She came home from Selfridges with the first pair of gloves. Black leather, perfectly practical. She knew she hadn't paid for them. She had a dim recollection of her right hand caressing the leather as she browsed idly on her lunch break. Found herself modelling the gloves when she returned to the office, the security tag somehow severed.

Next were the tiny diamond stud earrings. Her phantom hand had good taste; she'd grant it that. It was subtle, each steal a skillful manoeuvre. After a few weeks, Carrie found herself fascinated by its dexterity.

Eventually she was caught. The court was lenient in retrospect; they only charged her with the one offence and she was given a light sentence for a first offence on condition she do community service. Attend a therapy group to get post-traumatic support.

For the hand appears to be addicted to the thrill of theft.

'Would you like to introduce yourself, love?' Eileen's voice brings Carrie back to the present. She raises her hands to the circle so that people can see the crudity of the transplant scar. Ignores the now familiar muttering of surprise.

'I'm Carrie. I had a hand transplant. And my right hand is an addict.'

The Bone Queen

Nana Hannah was beating up a tempest on her bin lids. Utilising a spatula and a wooden spoon, her baggy arms worked overtime to pound noise across the scrap yard. Frankie and I paused abruptly at the threshold, his elbow sharp in my side watching her warily, knowing that the spatula was as likely to be taken to the backs of our legs as it was the lids.

The old tyrant's gaze located us despite the moonshine of age in her pupils. 'Patrick! Francis! Stop lurking and bring my smokes' she barked, arms pausing briefly.

Skulking past her into the cool shadow of her caravan, Frankie wordlessly handed me the scrappy leather baccie pouch and watched solemn faced as I concentrated over a roll up. I tilted my face around the silver doorsill, hand trembling just a little with the proffered fat cigarette just about holding together.

Hannah snatched it from my fingers, her spoon momentarily retired to the bench beside her. There was a film of sweat on her top lip; the magnificent moustache that lined it gleaming in the harsh afternoon sun of an Indian summer. As she pursed her mouth contentedly about the cigarette, I watched as her eyes close with deep satisfaction, a fleeting expression soon replaced by the more customary irritation.

One lunar eye opened. 'You got nothing to do, boy?' she hissed.

My response faltered; the eyes hardened.

'Get the trunk from the van. That useless brother of yours can help you carry it.'

Frankie slunk from the caravan door, his twig arms crossed pleadingly over his chest. Bad move. Nana Hannah abhorred idleness but she hated any hint of weakness more. Waving her spatula with renewed gusto, she let loose a stream of steaming vituperation unfit for any ten-year-old's ears, and we ran to please her lest the spatula run down upon our sunburnt legs.

We heaved the trunk to her, puny muscles straining to exist in our summer-stained arms. An unsophisticated black box coated with leather, it was a relic from another era. An era when the local children called her a totter and worse. A childhood from which she would recount fantastic tales about leading a pet fox on a lead to school. When she wore rags and castoffs from the neighbours whilst her parents' broiled bones for dog meat and profit. When holidays were spent following a red rag cart pulled by a piebald nag called Curly.

Curly's bones had long since become meat themselves and Nana Hannah's memories were cast in the pearly glow of youthful memory that omitted the death stench of bone render that had soaked indelibly into her clothing and hair, leading to her classmates nicknaming her the Bone Queen for her imperious manner.

Hannah leaned the trunk against the vast silver caravan that rose above the yard. Popping the lock, she grunted with satisfaction, rummaging inside before emerging with a whalebone corset of impossibly tiny circumference that swirled with tiny stars embroidered into the black silk. Catching us watching, she scrabbled at her money pouch and threw us a few small coins.

'Get some ice pops,' she grunted, an order rather than a kindness. Hannah wanted her privacy and we didn't hesitate to flee the dreadful old woman in preference for bright sugared water from Mr Chapman up the road.

Icepops in hand, we sat kicking our legs against the small wall at the side of their father's general store. The town spread out below us, hazy in heat that fermented a plague of insects; greenfly that spattered the back of our legs where we'd scratch them into insignificance. Other than the contented slurp of four blue icicles, late afternoon was quiet in the heat.

There came a steady clop of hooves behind us and unexpectedly our father trundled into view, a skewbald carthorse placidly dipping at his side. Pa Corrigan, his scrubby hair plastered flat to his skeletal cheekbones, boots clipping in time with the horse's gait. He eyed us laconically before gesturing to us to fall in behind him.

No questions asked, indeed fearing a clip, we obliged with the two Chapman boys following on our heels in breathless excitement. Silently, Pa led us downhill like the Pied Piper. The nag brought more small boys to the parade, a solemn gathering of children stepping carefully around cascades of pungent dung that fountained from that ginger rump.

Reaching the yard, Pa hooked the horse to an iron ring set beside the gate. Eight small boys now followed in silence.

Nana Hannah was sitting by her glittering caravan, her triumphant face carved ivory as she stood and twirled for Pa. She was wearing her corset cinched impossibly tight above a black dress stiff with formality that swirled about her ankles, the neck pulled up high in a frothy concoction of lace. A ghost of a smile passed Pa's face and he bowed to her, a gesture of respect so formal that instinctively all of us boys followed suit.

Pa turned and regarded Frankie and me inscrutably.

'Boys, get the cart for Nana.'

We exchanged uneasy glances. The cart had a carapace of garishly painted oak bound within a skeleton of steel, all carried on two flimsy wheels. It had stood ignored and unloved in the brick hut since before our births.

'Now!' he barked in sudden command.

It took a platoon of small boys but we managed it, firstly peeling back the shaking wooden doors to the outhouse and stabilising them against the wall with bricks. The shed was dimly lit and the dust stirred by skittering feet obscured the cart in a hazy sun dressed mist. I could hear the indrawn breath of my friends as they clustered about me gazing at the gaudy frame's dangerously long arms balanced upright on a wooden scaffold tower. Frankie sneezed with the dust, a small paw smearing a glistening trail of snot across his top lip. He walked to stand by a wheel as tall as him and wider by far, his pinched face beaming as he gazed up at the cracked leather seat at the head of the cart, a small rail rising from a foot well the only concession to safety.

I moved the wheel chucks, then carefully greased the joints with bike oil that clung to my fingers with a sour metallic tang. The platoon had faded into a blur of pale ovals in the doorway behind me, and I had to beckon them forward to assess their potential uses. I lined up three boys on either side and instructed them to firmly grasp the sharp poles that the horse would be harnessed to. I moved Frankie to stand by the door, not without protest. Then, with my heart skipping, I kicked the wooden tower holding the cart upright, leaving it to be supported by pure kid power.

There was a moment's silence; then a couple of sudden 'oufs!' as the weight of the cart settled on six sets of shoulders and dipped alarmingly to the right. Then twelve legs steadied and there was a sudden cheer as the cartwheels gave and momentum took the wooden centipede staggering forward towards Frankie. His hazelnut face cracked into a great smile and he shouted 'HEAVE!', asserting his position as my sergeant at arms.

Our grubby soldiers obliged, straining against the yellow paint of the cart arms, the wheels hesitant at first, then running smooth as they clicked into place and thirty years of inertia fell away. As it glided into the centre of the yard, Nana Hannah declared her delight with a resurgent pounding of the lids, her spatula head almost splintered from its pole and swinging wildly out of tune. Even Pa was smiling, his eyes creased against the sun. The horse ignored us all, tethered in the shadow of the wall with his head hanging in a half doze.

'Right, Hannah, let's get you back on the road' Pa bellowed.

An hour later the cart was dressed for its odyssey. Resplendent at the helm was Nana Hannah, her spatula replaced with a long leather whip which she fiercely brandished at any small hands that sought to pet the horse. The early evening sun caught on the silver stars of her corset and the flare of gypsy silver at her wrists and ears. Pa had changed from his usual totter's uniform of dusty pants and striped shirt, sleeves rolled to his elbows. Instead he stood in the baking heat in a three-piece suit with sweat already beading in the grooves on his forehead.

The yard fell silent, eight solemn boys forming an honour guard at the gate as Pa caught the nag's bridle and turned him gingerly towards the gate. The cart followed easily behind and Hannah crowed her delight, swaying her whip in time with the horse's gait.

As our ragged troop fell in behind the cart, it struck me how quiet the streets were. People were at their doors, the terrace full of curious eyes watching our progress. Men and women, babies clutching at their mother's pinafores; they all stood in silence as we walked slowly past. Some raised a hand in muted respect. Hannah soaked it up like a queen, her tobacco-ash hair crowning her with steely glory.

I knew my Nana Hannah for the first time ever that evening, I think. I watched her with reverence as she rode that cart; Boudicca supping whiskey from Pa's hip flask and spouting poetry with her reedy voice weak but determined. Kipling, Yeats, Blake; she invoked their spirits whilst calling out to a past as one reviled and yet forged hard in the filthy rag and bone shop of the past. Cars stopped as she passed, some dipping their lights to her passing. The honour guard of eight small boys in various states of cleanliness was ever in attendance, little Frankie staunchly keeping pace with the longer legs of his compadres.

The stout carthorse never balked, circling the entire estate willingly, as if aware that this was the closest to royalty he would ever be asked to carry. As for Pa, well he said nothing but he smiled occasionally.

Sadly.

Finally, we completed a full circuit of the estate as dusk fell and began to wind our way back up the steep terrace towards the yard.

Here our ranks grew, as the families of our small soldiers wordlessly slipped in behind us until we were fifty strong; mothers, daughters, fathers and toothless old men all following the indomitable spirit of an age long vanished. Someone had lit the fire barrels in the yard and we entered the battered gateway to bright flares of warmth and the makings of a street party.

I saw my Nana Hannah for the last time ever that evening. Frankie and I hid at the edges, dizzy with delight to be allowed such a late night. The lingering revellers left the yard under the stars at the witching hour. Hannah refused to come indoors so Pa made her up a bed in the back of the wagon where she could gaze rheumily towards a buttermilk summer moon.

At some point that night she simply followed it, her spirit spiralling loose and free towards the stars whilst her earthly form lay cocooned in the very place that she'd been conceived. When Frankie and I stumbled outside, yawning at a sticky dawn, we found Pa sat at the back of the cart, staring into a mug of tarry tea as a silent reservoir of tears caught in the corners of his mouth before dropping to pool on his formal white shirt. Hannah made gold and silver from rags; music from tin bins and broken utensils. She recycled Kipling like she recycled other people's refuse. The Bone Queen passed; and a man once a boy still makes his prayer to a rag, a bone and a hank of hair.

The Ghost Induction

'You've forgotten your feet.'

Daniel's tone was stern. Marina gathered her manners and bit back a retort as she worked on the finer details of materialisation. Feet were the least of her worries.

Take clothes, for example. She'd thought of going for something a little modern, a little streamlined. A cream blouse, perhaps, with a pearl and garnet brooch at the throat. The image was there, perfectly crafted in her mind. Yet when it came to execution, the result was always the same. A wedding dress. Cream brocade, demure bodice with seed pearls at the neck, and a froth of Chantilly lace.

Daniel was perched on the pulpit, lips pursed as he swung his legs through the wood. Marina refrained from mentioning his own missing feet; in the short time she'd inhabited this otherworld she had found that politeness was the path best taken. She was also figuring out that how one wished to look when materialised didn't necessarily correspond with the end result. The mind seemed to default to the burial outfit. And some fool had gussied her up in a wedding outfit.

Lieutenant Daniel Jay was still giving Marina a critical overview. He'd lost his cap and his feet but his bearing was still militaristic. He'd been a bonny lad in his day; dark hair and round eyes that should have been smiling. Marina endured the scrutiny without comment. A vicar's daughter tends to learn patience at a very early age.

So, she donned her cream slippers and slipped up to join him behind the altar from where they could observe the ceremony without obstruction. Proximity to the living tended to make all involved uncomfortable.

'What are you doing, Miss Marina?'

Daniel was polite but sounded a little perplexed. Marina had been twisting in midair, following a ray of sun as it gleamed on the gold lain at the high altar. She gave a guilty twitch, turning to face him.

The sun made her almost translucent, her hair spun the palest of flax as it formed a halo about her face.

'Were you looking at your reflection?' He was amused, she noted, the left corner of his mouth forming a dimple.

She had been trying to, twisting across the surface of a heavy golden chalice wondering how death had marked her face. She'd found no reflection, no matter how hard she had tried. Perhaps she herself was the reflection, she thought morbidly.

She crossed her arms, set her mouth and glowered at him mutely. It appeared that in death her every move was to be shadowed by this politely amused young man. So much for eternal slumber.

'I was curious' she muttered, turning away from him and ascending towards the stone vaults of the nave. 'I just wondered – *you* know?'

Daniel was silent but she felt him materialising at her side.

'I wondered if I'd come back whole' she muttered. If she'd had blood vessels, her cheeks would have been rosy.

An uncomfortable silence fell between them; then, as the noon bells began to peel, Daniel answered very quietly.

'You're perfectly formed, Miss Marina. A little pale in your finery perhaps. But —'

Intrigued by his hesitation, Marina stepped from her ledge and met his eyes as she stood unthinkingly on air. 'But?'

'You're like an old watercolour. Beautiful in the execution but fading with exposure to light.'

As she understood his words, Marina felt the air letting her go. Allowed herself to fade with it, into the grey stones beneath the nave. Down into the earth where quieter bones than hers lay in their tattered raiment.

Marina stayed in the soothing darkness of the crypt, visiting her neighbours in the soft light of her own eldritch glow. This was a Norman cathedral and the crypt held its oldest residents. Most were quiet now; mere forms of bone and rag, the occasional gleam of gold on a finger or a jewel that caught her passing light and that for one brief moment would glow with ghostly beauty.

There were few souls remaining and those that were had faded to voiceless sepia.

There was little sense of time as Marina cast her light, a beautiful firefly without purpose. Burning long after she should have been extinguished.

Marina never could say what impulse had drawn her skyward that dull day. All she knew was that it was no longer enough to haunt the dark, staring at her slippers.

Shadows marked the aisle as she made her way down to the font. She ignored the warmth and scent of live bodies drifting beneath her as she walked the air above their heads. These massed worshippers in their sombre finery; the altar boys in their crimson were of no importance to her, their noise jarring after the silence of the sepia ghosts.

Human stillness drew her to the tranquility of the Lady Chapel where she found a man, head bowed before a book of remembrance, his hands resting on his knees as he settled on a knitted hassock.

Those hands. Long, supple fingers, calloused and brown, nails squared off bluntly. Whorls of dried skin on the knuckles; a bracelet crafted from a thin dried leather strap wrapped round the right wrist three times and knotted crudely, two blue beads hanging on the plaited braid.

Marina reached perplexed fingers to the beads then shot roofwards with shock as she made physical contact for the first time since her passing. She recalled the beads daintily suspended from earrings on curved golden stems that allowed them to swing freely from her earlobes.

Perched at the top of the stone window arch she fruitlessly swiped at her ears to get a sense of what hung there now. She could ask Daniel. She doubted he'd tell her without a lengthy sermon on vanity.

From here she could see the top of the stranger's head, his ears pink whorls close into the skull, the blond hair shaved close to the neck. She pulled her knees to her chin, an incongruous shade hovering in the pale light, her focus entirely on the man below her.

The man never raised his head, so still that only the movement of his chest told her he was still breathing, his head bowed before the small altar of the Lady Chapel.

Marina felt Daniel materialise beside her.

'Who is he?'

'I'm...I don't know. He feels familiar but I just can't quite grasp it.' Marina felt woeful, her memory full of holes.

Beside her Daniel nodded sadly. 'It happens like that. The memories, the good ones seem so patchy. Sometimes I think it's a blessing. Stops us regretting.'

There seemed little Marina could say to that so she hung in silence watching the rainbow colours from the stained-glass windows fading into shade on the man's face.

The three observed their vigil until the cathedral verger began his circuit, lighting candles to flicker softly on the altar. With a sigh and nod to him, the living man rose and walked a solitary path that the ghosts could not follow.

Marina remembered what it had felt like to dance. In her polite small society, the opportunity to do so happened infrequently, every chance eagerly seized upon.

She would glide across the floor in pale blue slippers, allowing herself to be held very lightly and without the slightest hint of misappropriation. All the while she would be fizzing with joy inside, the freedom of her feet a guilty pleasure.

She was thinking of this when the blond man returned. Time had a dreamy quality within the cathedral; who could say whether it was a day, a month, even a year after she'd first found him in the Lady Chapel.

Her path through the air led inexorably to him, to kneel beside him with her hands clasped on her knee as she turned a timid gaze to his profile.

Dark blond lashes sat on pale skin, his eyes cast down to his hands. If he was praying, he was doing so silently. The blue beads still hung from his wrist, suspended now from a loose gold bracelet.

Marina remembered the feel of those beads as they'd caught her neck as she danced, a little clumsy in her inexperience. She remembered a man —

this man — smiling at her as he'd swung her round, her earrings brushing against her neck.

As Marina's shade watched the living man, he sat up, palms flat on his knees as he gazed at the window. Pale light slanted through it, infusing them with dancing shapes of blue and purple.

Tentatively she reached out a hand, letting pale fingers sweep across the man's cheek as she noticed the constellation of freckles there. 'The great bear' she'd called him, after the pattern they formed.

She remembered that same constellation pressed against her cheek as he'd swung her round the dance floor, his grip a little tighter, her head a little woozy for the wine she'd drunk and the feel of his hand against the small of her back. Her shoes were white with tiny pearls for button clasps.

There was a long white lace hem brushing her ankles, a tight bodice fastened with seed pearls to match her shoes. The shoes she was wearing right now, she realised with some distress. The blond man dressed in a sober dark suit; white shirt with little rounded collar.

Marina remembered his name: Johannes. She'd met him as she helped her father minister the Danish Bethel, serving broth and strong tea to the soldiers billeted far from home on strange shores. They'd stumbled over language, their speech foreign to the other but the day she had tripped while carrying a tray and he had caught her hands to steady her, Marina had realised that there was another language in which they were fluent. Saw her thoughts reciprocated in his warm smile as he'd set her back on her feet, those gentle hands cradling her own.

She had married Johannes in this very cathedral on a day when she'd felt like dancing on the cold stone flagstones, forgetting that the casts of the dead lay beneath her feet as sober reminders of what all must become.

Marina's hand sat against Johannes' cheek. As she did so, he turned his face to hers breathing her name. He spoke the words he had whispered on their wedding day, words that she thought she would never lose, but had misplaced in death:

'I love you for all that you are, all that you have been, and all that you are yet to be.'

Marina sought solace in the crypt, obsessing over the fraying threads in her mind that connected her to Johannes. She was aware that Daniel often visited her, hovering on the edge of her consciousness.

Time was fluid as the two ghosts circled each other warily, unwilling to disturb old bones.

Eventually Marina followed Daniel skyward again, finding him sitting atop a pew next to a brass plaque set into the nave wall. She realised suddenly that she no longer noticed the absence of feet. Instead she focused on the steadiness of his face.

She sat beside him, crossing her ankles daintily as she squinted at the brass a little ashamed she'd never taken the time to read them sooner.

Fifteen words to describe a life. To date a death.

'Mine' he said, in answer to her unspoken query.

She'd breathed for three years more than him. That struck her as hard. She'd only been gifted twenty-three of them. This gently spoken young man had spent his twentieth year on the Somme. Lost his life there before she'd even been born.

She voiced her thoughts.

Daniel shrugged. 'It was a life. Some folk got less. They didn't talk about it but many of the young lads barely scraped fifteen.'

Marina looked down, focused on the air where his feet should have been. Noted that someone had taken the trouble to pin his trousers closed over the wounds. Realised with sorrow that someone had loved this young man once, much as she'd been loved in life.

'Like I say, the memories are hazy,' he continued. 'But I had a sweetheart like you.'

'Does she visit?'

'She wasn't the sort to dwell on loss, Marina. Practical. I remember that. I remember that and I can't even remember the colour of her eyes.'

Marina found her fingers linking with Daniel's as they sat side by side, both staring at the void where his feet should have been. Neither commented on how solid they felt in each other's clasp. They never spoke of his sweetheart again.

The ghosts lost time as they explored the cathedral, finding beauty in unexpected places. The delicate structures of rodent skulls in the crypt, the observation that the sepia ghosts would dance in time with the music from above, their hazy lights a murmuration in the gloom.

It seemed that Daniel's light grew brighter as Marina came to know him, their hands unconsciously entwined as they shimmered amongst the flags of wars long gone to dust that hung in the entrance hall.

Johannes still visited on occasion, a little greyer, a little more stooped each time. The grey of his hair was the only measure left to Marina to gauge the passage of time. Daniel would withdraw discreetly during these visits, allowing Marina to join Johannes at his vigil in the Lady Chapel.

She would join Johannes side by side in vigil but she never endeavoured to touch him again.

There came a bright day one late winter when Marina and Daniel were amusing themselves by painting the ghostly tones of their skins with rainbow lights from the great stained-glass windows that formed the base of the nave. Marina favoured purple, swirling it through the loose mass of her pale hair as she danced on air.

Daniel preferred not to dance but would stream at speed from one beam of light to another, painting himself a rainbow of blues, ochre and crimson.

In a moment everything changed. Marina felt it deep inside of herself, a piercing wrench of grief in which she felt time sigh. Daniel had been laughing as he'd played, but seeing her hanging motionless, he headed straight to her side where she could not, would not look at him. Would not see the grief and sorrow that darkened his eyes as Daniel realised before Marina what had come to pass.

They ghosted to the Lady Chapel, Marina filled with an urgency she didn't understand, barely aware of Daniel fading a little at her side.

There she saw him. Johannes, his sailor's cap in his hand as he stood rumpling his hair, her blue beads dangling still at his wrist. Saw him turning in confusion towards her as his bemused eyes widened as she came to a halt before his face.

She saw Johannes before her in death, his shade uncertain even as she watched joy blossom on his face.

Marina did not see Daniel withdrawing to the door, loss etching itself deeply into his pale face.

'Marina?' Joahnnes' voice was a rasp. 'Marina? It can't be —'

'It can' she whispered. 'It is. Oh, my love.'

As she stepped towards him, he held out his broad hands and she saw her beads gleaming in the winter light. All of her being, all of her soul was infused with light and love as she stepped forward and clasped his hand as he laughed and swung her into a happy dance, letting her lead him up, up, up into the brilliant play of colour in the windows.

Husband and wife lifted their faces in awe as the light deepened about them; then stepped into the palm of the painted Christ. Together they coalesced into a ball of incandescent light that seared into the heart-sore gaze of the young soldier left behind once more. Left to fade alone into his memorial of brass and stone awaiting the next lost soul to find him.

The Repository of Lost Souls: Where They Came From

Every story has a place where it begins, and mine are no exception. Writing workshops are a great place to ferment ideas that can take you in unanticipated directions. Here's a short background to my Lost Souls.

1	**El Salto Del Colacho**
	El Salto del Colacho (The Devil's Jump) is a traditional Spanish festival dating back to 1620 that takes place annually to celebrate the Catholic feast of Corpus Christi in Castrillo de Murcia. During the festival, known as El Salto del Colacho (the devil's jump) or El Colacho, men dressed as the Devil (known as the Colacho) in red and yellow suits jump over babies born during the previous twelve months of the year who lie on mattresses in the street. The 'devils' hold whips and oversized castanets as they jump over the infant children.
	The Colacho jumps over the babies on the mattresses placed on the procession route traversing the town. The origins of the tradition are unknown but it is said to cleanse the babies of original sin, ensure them safe passage through life and guard against illness and evil spirits.
	This story came from a workshop themed on festivals hosted by the wonderful Jennifer C. Wilson.
2	**Follow the Hare**
	The same workshop asked us to consider developing a story themed on a significant calendar event without referencing its name in the written work. I chose Easter, and from there my small girl became enchanted with following the hare when searching for eggs. What she finds isn't quite what she expected.

3	**Sister Vampire**
	Not all vampires are wicked. Meet little Thessaly, with her wisps of hair and demon face pulling. And a brother who likes to lick windows. This story took me a while to write and underwent numerous incarnations before reaching you here. I live by the sea and feel that yearning to soar on the thermals on the worst of days. To be free. But I'll stick to letting the dog lick the windows!
4	**Barflies**
	A workshop in the wonderful Moniack Mhor asked us to think about place in terms of how it feels underfoot, how it smells. To use the senses. I lived above a village public house between the ages of five and nine. It took me back to roaming the bar, drinking more sugar than was perhaps wise and that sense of the bar waiting to reopen in the late afternoon sun as the dust played down the drafts in the lounge. Some spaces travel with you for life. Barflies is based on that space. I really did harvest all the money behind the banquettes and spent it on rainbow sherbet, Sindy doll clothes and hardcover Enid Blyton books.
5	**Blood Poppies / The Memory Tin**
	In 2014, I began to research my family history. This led me to an interest in the Great War, a century from its beginnings. I attended World War 1 themed workshops hosted by the Tyne and Wear Archives at Segedunum Roman Fort in Wallsend and in The Discovery Museum in Newcastle. Here I handled artifacts from the Great War including a tin gifted by Princess Mary to the troops overseas. This tin wove its way into two pieces of very short fiction – *Blood Poppies* and *The Memory Tin*, which are paired in this book as they are both about the same person, and started as one story. Sometimes we wear our past on our faces. I have a similar scar on my own chin, from a dog bite. That's another story, for another day.

6	**Longshanks and Lavender**
	Written with the lovely Linskill Writers. The brief was to write a seasonal story in my local area. The month was May and I remembered how I used to revise for my 'A' Levels with the sash windows open watching the world (and the boys) go by. Lila drifted into my mind in a haze of purple hair. Scott was smitten as he saw her passing by.
	Many of my stories have a paranormal twist to them, and Shellycoat came from reading Dee Chainey's *A Treasury of British Folklore: Maypoles, Mandrakes and Mistletoe*. A shellycoat is a bogeyman wearing a coat covered in shells that rattle when he moves. They wander around lakes and rivers in Northern England and Scotland.
	An early version of this story was published by in a pamphlet with The Linskill Writers group in 2018.
7	**Nymphae and Neridae**
	My freshwater undines (mermaids). Twins torn apart by a beautiful human voice that drifts into their solitude on the wind. I was creating character studies for a possible novel when the sisters became flesh in my mind. Nymphae remains angry. I see her in her pool, hair drifting on the surface, a temptation to the unwary. Beware the siren's song!
8	**Private 48196**
	Private 48196 won 3rd place in Story Tyne 2014 and came from a workshop run by North Tyneside Library Services. It was written in memory of my great uncle, Michael Maughan Renwick, who died in April 1918 aged just seventeen. Michael was just one of the estimated 250,000 boy soldiers who fought for their country in the Great War. *Star stuff, harvesting sunshine (Carl Sagan).*

9	**The Carousel Queen**
	A story I wrote to celebrate the restoration of the beautiful Whitley Bay Dome in my hometown, restored to its former glory. May there be many joyful moments in its future.
10	**The Consequential Hand**
	A runner-up in Story Tyne 2016. I became a little obsessed with the idea of a 'bad hand' after hearing the Gilmore and Roberts song, *The Stealing Arm*. Carrie is a modern-day version, with her perfect coat, pristine gloves and unlawful compulsions.
11	**The Bone Queen**
	Highly commended in the Red Squirrel Press inaugural Sara Park Memorial Prize in 2012 – an earlier version of this story was published in the prize pamphlet at this time. Hannah was inspired by a mix of poetry and imagery, and memories of a heat wave summer when the tarmac melted and the ladybirds overflowed their boundaries. It is also the name of my paternal Grandmother, of whom I have very little memory but who, from what I have heard, was rather a character.
12	**The Ghost Induction**
	Marina and Daniel, ghosts of different eras. I volunteered on a research and writing project, *Reflections of Newcastle 1914–1918*, to help write three interactive e-books that looked at how the Great War impacted on Newcastle upon Tyne as a city. As part of my research, I visited the Anglican Cathedral, St Nicholas, to study the war memorials. I fell in love with it and have revisited it several times since. I love the beautiful Danish window dedicated to the sailors billeted on the Tyne, one of whom weaves his heart into this story.

Finally, with thanks to...

The people I love and cherish have filtered into this little book at every stage. I can't thank you all enough for you love and support in keeping me going. You know who you are, but here are a few hugs as a reminder.

North Tyneside Writers' Circle and North Tyneside Libraries for writing prompts, encouragement, and writing and book gossip post circle, occasionally fuelled by something a little stronger than tea! A collective hug to the whole circle including organisers Elaine Cusack (aka the Princess of Felling), Sandy Chadwin and...

...My writing big sister Jennifer C. Wilson who occasionally has to pull me down from the procrastination ledge and back behind my desk!

Penny Blackburn – amazing poet and Circle companion. Yes, I remember my promise to buy that bottle of champagne made foolishly at the Dome! One day that novel will come.

My Virtual Crew – aka the nicest people I have never met. Simon Brew, Louisa Mellor, Rosie Fletcher, Paul Childs and all those who stop by and say hello to me on the Twitter writing community. You can join us @Gingerdolly

Heather Turner – Don't Dream It, Be It! Just please don't ever turn my face green again.

Fiona Thompson – for being a doll and offering to proofread the final version of this book when I'd gone word blind! Thanks for saving my sanity.

My family: Mam & Bill; David & Corrina; Jessica & Aunty Elsie.

Last but never least, Paul Roberts-Morpeth, my beautiful man. Thank you for your constant belief in me, and for your strength, kindness and perpetual love. You are the star by which my compass is set. Jack & I love you xxx

Printed in Great Britain
by Amazon